C.

P9-DUU-795

Nicholas Heller

HAPPY BIRTHDAY, MOE DOG

Greenwillow Books, New York

LIBRARY OF CONGRESS CATALOGING-IN-PUBLICATION DATA

HELLER, NICHOLAS.   HAPPY BIRTHDAY, MOE DOG.
SUMMARY: ALL THE LETTERS THAT SPELL HAPPY BIRTHDAY
HELP MOE DOG ENJOY HIS BIRTHDAY.
[1. BIRTHDAYS—FICTION.   2. DOGS—FICTION]   I. TITLE.
PZ7.H37426HAP   1988   [E]   87-14851
ISBN 0-688-07670-X   ISBN 0-688-07671-8 (LIB. BDG.)

WATERCOLORS, ACRYLIC PAINTS AND INK
WERE USED FOR THE FULL-COLOR ART.
THE TEXT TYPE IS ITC KORINNA.

COPYRIGHT © 1988 BY NICHOLAS HELLER
ALL RIGHTS RESERVED. NO PART OF THIS BOOK
MAY BE REPRODUCED OR UTILIZED IN ANY FORM
OR BY ANY MEANS, ELECTRONIC OR MECHANICAL,
INCLUDING PHOTOCOPYING, RECORDING OR BY
ANY INFORMATION STORAGE AND RETRIEVAL
SYSTEM, WITHOUT PERMISSION IN WRITING
FROM THE PUBLISHER, GREENWILLOW BOOKS,
A DIVISION OF WILLIAM MORROW & COMPANY, INC.,
105 MADISON AVENUE, NEW YORK, N.Y. 10016.
PRINTED IN HONG KONG BY SOUTH CHINA PRINTING CO.
FIRST EDITION   10 9 8 7 6 5 4 3 2 1

FOR MY PARENTS

The alarm went off, and Moe Dog woke up.

There was an **H** at the foot of his bed.

"Happy Birthday, Moe Dog," it said.

"What a lovely day it is."

Moe Dog looked out his window. The sun was shining, and a large **A** was flapping around the house. "Happy Birthday!" it shouted as it passed by.

"Come along downstairs," said the **H**.
"The **P**'s are preparing your breakfast."

There they were in the kitchen frying eggs.

"Sit right down, Moe Dog," they said.

"As it is your birthday, we will wait on you."

During breakfast a Y and a B arrived,
carrying a large trunk.

"Look, here is a splendid birthday suit for you, Moe Dog," said the Y.

"But first you must have a bath," said the B.

So after breakfast Moe Dog had
a birthday bubble bath.

And then he got dressed in his new birthday clothes.
"You look pretty sharp, Moe Dog," said the Y.

The next to arrive was an I,
and it too was carrying a box.

"Happy birthday, Moe Dog," it said.

"This is a crown for you to wear,

because today you are the king."

As all the letters gathered around to admire Moe Dog
in his wonderful birthday outfit, there came a loud
knocking on the door, and someone began shouting.

It was an **R**.

"Help, come quickly!" it said. "The birthday
tent has collapsed on the **T**!"

"What will we do?" All the letters began shouting
  at once.

"I know," said Moe Dog. "The **A** can lift up the tent."

"Where am I?" cried the T. "Oh, here I am.
Happy birthday, Moe Dog!"

"I hope we're not late," called an **H** and
a **D** as they came running up. "We have
your birthday presents, Moe Dog."

"And we have the birthday cake,"
said an **A** and a **Y**, hurrying up
from the other direction.

"Now we're all here," the letters
shouted, "and the party can begin.
Happy birthday, Moe Dog!"

They danced and played all day, until

it was time for Moe Dog to shut

his eyes, make a birthday wish,

and blow out the candles on his cake.